Songs of Neglect

Who will change the old narratives?

Owonam Umana Ebong

Songs of Neglect

"Are we orphans in any way? Have we been ridiculed? Who among these groups are illegitimate? The parents who brought children to the world without planning or the innocent children who came by them without a choice? If women can give birth to royalty, then what is royalty without women? What is the striking difference or features of a commoner and the throne apart from the crown? What is the value of the throne without the commoners that will cheer the crown? The crown does not speak to heights but commoners. Commoners are the strength of every throne. I think it's only possible for royalty to rule over the commoners, not another royalty. Commoners are as crucial as royalty, though they are not royalty but if they revolt and make themselves royalty, they are royalty because they can choose especially when their pains are unbearable."

DEDICATION

I gladly Dedicate this book to God almighty, whose inspiration I have enjoyed and my very supportive wife.

CHAPTER ONE

"…adieu," screamed an intense crackled voice, wiping dusty breeze off his eyelids, confusedly yawning severally as tears and sticky mucus dropped from his nostrils. He sneezed strongly, looking at every frightening particle of the quiet cemetery propelled by the wind from place to place with some hash dry sounds as if someone were walking on dry leaves. His hope crashed as he continually stared at every seemingly moving image as the partial light of the relenting moon shadowed with ease on every nearby tree. The environment was very solemn due to different teasing sounds of insects that made him feel he was still on earth. Cold breeze penetrated softly like ice water to the tooth, but he did not bother about it because he was used to that kind of situation.

"You didn't try enough for me..."

Clearing his cracked voice, Green touched and cleaned dust particles from the coarse surfaces of both tombs, which laid together with an inch gap as if they were sharing the same grave. The tombs were arranged horizontally with different flowers on most of them, differentiating the poor from the rich. There was no separate location for social status, yet the contents and the type of stone made the difference. The small spaces between each stone baffled some people and made them ponder repeatedly whether they could be compared with those buried in their houses, compounds and private or family cemetery in luxury spaces. Well, maybe we should try harder to reduce those spaces. With the overcrowded population of people globally, it may be difficult to find enough space to bury the dead in time, or maybe old stones should be removed for new ones, or the government should introduce cremation into law to have space for agriculture and other development. If this happens, what about the dangers of the crematorium, the effect of high temperature of the furnace, exhaust from industrial ovens, the presence of chlorofluorocarbon, which can contribute to ozone layer depletion? What about the release of toxic minerals like mercury in the atmosphere, the presence of high acid-based chemicals, which could lead to cancer in laboratory animals, environmental hazards, and others.? I think the dangers involved in cremation would instead threaten and increase death rates and affect our environment negatively. Hmm! this is confusing as air without direction!

As most people would say, "you will know the rich man's death by his casket, tomb, announcement, mourners, testimonies of friends and the type of food and drinks served in his funeral. In any case, I guess six feet is six feet for all, same depth, no matter the decoration though some are burnt and thrown into the river or molded into beads, some preserved in the laboratory for experiments and some with no landing force. Well, for me, death is death, but the question is, where are you going after death? Hmm! Many people would sing, "man die go woman born another", but to some which you may not agree with, "there is life after death", which Jesus has introduced and given us victory over sin and death. Anywhere, death is inevitable.

Green continued, "you took pleasure in bringing me into this world to be disgraced, frustrated, disappointed and smashed to the ground like grains, abandoning the search you both happily initiated but leaving me in this deadly confused state with no hands to cuddle. What were you thinking? You know grandma is not rich at all, even when dosed in her long-forsaken hovel filled with rats, ants, cockroaches, termites, and their excrement. They never whisper but frighten strongly; I still find it difficult to breathe in my dreadful dreams to overcome these hurdles, just like grandma fights with her brothers who would never count her as a member of the family. Indeed, traditions are stupidity when fools are leaders. Life is a mirage, a library full of books without names for easy descriptions, an amusement park that does not excite. So why am I here?" He released more tears and cried steadily for a while.

The tombs were arranged horizontally with short gaps without reference to the slave or free born, but he agonized with pauses inviting the scary stones for response yet with no fear to ponder on. His heart was too heavy to let go quickly, especially when he saw other children playing with their parents, eating together, sharing stories and he had none.

"You left with the same rings you

bought, and you never allowed me a chance to suck your milk, feel your warmth, and be cuddled to sleep as nature had arranged. I wish I had the opportunity to have fatherly advice from dad before his demise. My birth is full of tears and regrets. Why should I come alone to stay with many that do not care or look-alike, though with the same language? I think hell could be better. How can I survive in a thick forest of life as cruel as this? Even the buttress roots are so huge and scary to sit on. I wonder what amazes animals to jump from one trunk to another! Maybe they have parents who watch and stops them from falling. The story of your death crippled me with no chance to notice your innocent faces. It is indeed a shame, a super story I would never stop sharing in tears".

He cleaned his watery eyes though more tears were flooding with ease, and he continued. "I would always come to this cemetery for companionship with skulls. How I wish these thousand tombs could teach me the best techniques and add more knowledge for survival in the world. I know there is absolutely nothing in this world wishing me good. My tears are food that satisfies though I still feel hungry. Now I know promises are deceptive; they are cruel when not activated. They are no clothes to feel warmer than parents; I hate you like snakes."

Green walked around the graves in the cemetery, kicking different sizes of dry leaves that created a more whamming effect but the anguish of such irreplaceable loss of his parents all in a day vexed his spirit such that he could fight with death for revenge. His parents were very vivacious in their planning towards the future, but their plans all somersaulted, thwarting their intelligent efforts, and incarcerated them from the surface of the earth.

"Oh! What an incapacitated and insane world I have found myself without consciousness. "Who can help me out of its venom"

As he was still complaining in the lonely cemetery, rats, cockroaches, and lizards were frightened as they came by though always alerted to detect strange movement for defense. The cemetery rats usually paraded in and out of every hole. Sometimes, he would watch these rats playing with each other and it helped put his sorrows away for some good minutes. Though most times, he wished they would understand, he felt more like a friend playing with them. At the same time, birds on most of his visiting days won't hesitate to keep him company too with their different feeding mouth paths, attractive colors, and feathers with their beautiful and pretty eyes.

While he was still observing the environment, his grandmother walked in with her walking stick. When she saw him at a reasonable distance near his parents' graves, she sat immediately on one of the graves muttering.

"Why wasn't it I that died than my children?

for homage to have it statutory importance,

Children would swim with courage.

Giving credits to nature, with good
memories to recount

A remarkable genealogy with flowers."

She paused and stared at nearby trees
and continued

"Sometimes, I ponder at the cruel
nature of death.

Owing no pity or apology to any

I wished I had not been born with
positive dreams.

Though none of the dreams had been
fulfilling than bitterness.

You are the only intruder to my soul.

Separating joy from pervading my
heart

Presenting huge suicidal questions with

dull memories,

Lubricating partnership with graves

An endless deep, I cannot comprehend.

Hmm...!

How can I sing this un- lucid melodious rhythm to an innocent, curious lad?"

Indeed, I am greatly deceived and exploited; yes, I am....

She scattered her hair as her rumpled head gear dropped hopelessly. More tears flooded down her chin, but she hurriedly cleaned them up to avoid critical questions from her sensitive grandson, who will never stop asking questions.

"Hey! Son. Its grandma. Jump up; it's

time to go home." She waved her stick in the air for easy identification. "Wow….! You are here again, grandma." Rats and birds dispersed from their relentless playground hiding with their glittering eyes spreading for defense as he stood up and shouted. "Oh! Sorry guys, I'll be back another day. Take care of my parents, bye" he greeted and walked away slowly to his grandmother, getting ready to be scolded by her because of his attitude of visiting the cemetery than the church.

"My Green," grand ma'am called. "You look a little brighter today, but why do you purposefully present this same agony every passing day? When will you forget about this cemetery and fix yourself on something important?" "I'm sorry grandma, but can't I see my parents at least once in life? Don't they love me as you confessed, or is it you alone that cares?" Green questioned with concern. "You are only but a child, my son. Your parents loved and would always love you as they agreeably brought you into this world...."

"No... Grand ma'am." Green interrupted loudly and walked few paces from her. "This world means no friend and is full of deceit. I am surrounded with people that say no words to comfort my heart." "Yes, son, it is true", his grand ma'am confirmed. Absolutely, but we have nothing to contribute other than to live in it silently while it allows us to breathe. But in all these, son, our God can change every situation." "Look at you with no helper grand ma'am, see your grey hairs which should be nurtured in smiles have gone in solitude because of tears. Is this how it should be?"

Green, she adjusted to gain more strength. "I dare not give praise to grey hairs than the words of wisdom it utters. The danger of seeing it on young people these days intoxicates me tremendously because they will certainly look like their parents. Instead, I yearn for wisdom to survive the waves, for it could be more costly than diamond though not priced in the market by merchants. What grey hairs offer these days have deteriorated in content. Most grey hairs keep on making silly decisions that enslave the commoners like us", the old woman explained.

"Grand ma'am, could malnutrition cause grey hairs on young people making them assume, they had arrived without passing through hard ways for experiences and knowledge?" I think this could be an insult to the elderly". "Son, you would have answers as you grow up. Grey hair is like wisdom which you must understand and desire in life." She explained calmly.

"Well… if that is the case, I'll pray not to have any grey hair." Green concluded ignorantly. "No, my son, his grand ma'am disagreed strongly. "Listen, there are so many in life struggle that did not pass through what I've experienced. I pray for you today, that with the help of God, you'll be among them someday." "Thank you, grand ma'am." He smiled and embraced her. "You are proudly welcome my son. Should we go now?" "Yes, grand ma'am."

They played and walked side by side discussing towards the entrance of the cemetery. Birds amazed them the more; singing repeatedly; mounting on one another; spreading their wings as they jumped from one trunk to another. Their activity frightened rats, while cockroaches were afraid of lizards by running into possible hiding places. The ants moved uniformly and later scattered in different directions looking for food. Generally, the ecological niche and food chain within the cemetery was amazing as they depended on one another for food.

CHAPTER TWO

On different occasions, grand ma'am went for morning prayers in the church without Green because he was very sluggish after waking up from sleep, and the distance to the church propelled the older woman to mind her business. She used an old lantern to see the road clearly till she meets up with other members of the church who were also going for the morning prayers.

One of the mornings, when grand ma'am did not return, Green hurriedly went to the stream to fetch some water for the house several times to impress her and to visit his entertainers at the cemetery, knowing how happy he will be after each sober exercise. Unfortunately, Grand ma'am overstayed, and Green was disturbed especially because he was hungry as this made him feel uneasy.

"Oh…. Mmaeyen Udo Umana Ekpo Eno! Whoop…" she called her names loudly and dropped her broom when she remembered that she didn't serve her grandson breakfast till that time of the day because of how lengthy the women's meeting was after morning prayers.

Grand ma'am rushed like wind home with her quenched lantern, wondering if Green had gone to his usual place without eating. But while entering her hovel she was surprised to see rats and lizard's excrement packed outside. She stretched her neck to have a good glance through the room. She saw Green's displeasing posture on the floor. She drew herself near him, trying to find out what could emanate such unusual sleep to an active young boy at that time of the day. Still, Green could not say anything, he rather looked at her faintly, breathing so slowly because he was feebly inactive while tears were dropping from his eyes.

Grand ma'am understanding such trying atmosphere, forgot tying up her falling wrappers but hurriedly made and offered him some sugar and salt in water to drink; she also gave him some fruits to boost his strength before eating solid food. As grand ma'am was preparing breakfast, Green was revived and could wait patiently to eat the food. Green went to the cemetery with some fruits and bread grand ma'am gave him as it became his hobby to always visit the cemetery, cry on his parents' grave and watch his creeping animal friends dash into the holes for safety. He sat on his mother's thumb and dropped his belonging on his father's. He repeatedly stirred at the tree trunks as the comforting breeze was blowing softly to offer friendship to the vulnerable. He munched his bread aggressively owing no regret or apology to the hungry rats and lizards though still stirring at them as if he was protecting his territory as well. His frightening eyes couldn't scare them away entirely from their un-whole-some character. Rats and lizards saw and wished to have been as small as ants to eat from the crumbs without noticing as they couldn't grasp opportunity such as that. Green acted as if he read through their minds and threw food a bit far away from him though he did not respond immediately to their repeated glances. He saw some of the rats walked away, scratching their black tails by a nearby stone while others somewhat diverted their attention from him, lizards also were displaying an oscillatory movement. The birds maturely were minding their businesses, jumping from one place to another. These things in the environment impressed Green a lot. When he had regained strength fully, he threw some leftovers to them without knowing rats already knew what he would do before rushing the meal.

The case of his interaction with rats, birds, and lizard interests him graciously such that he spontaneously wished to be with them constantly because he did not know any other place as rewarding as the cemetery despite being taken to church by his grandma severally. Green was not active in any children's programs in the church, even when his grandma had advised and encouraged him to do so. He felt distraught and angry when parents would appreciate their children during recitation, songs, and drama during children church programs. As a result, most children could not get close to him, neither did he go to them.

Whenever Green visited the cemetery, he forgot his sorrows while watching these animals move from place to place, eating, playing, and fighting each other. They were never attacked yet they would hurriedly observe and defend themselves at any sound or intrusion. Their intelligence taught him suitable lessons about a life full of uncertainties, friendship, intruding enemy like death and the need for adjustment for survival.

Unfortunately, his grand ma'am died and Green who was trying to recover from the death of his parents, went into grief again and got involved in different responsibilities to eat at least a meal in a day since his last provider passed away. He still spent most of his time crying his heart out at the cemetery and returned home very late some days to sleep. Nobody was concerned or ready to bear the responsibility of feeding or taking care of him. This was not so strange because he knew how difficult it was for his grandmother to have support and feed him three times a day when she was alive.

In the evening, her grandmother's family members who were still alive gathered before he could return to the battered hovel. "Hey! Rundown here quickly." One of his mothers' uncles Hector commanded repulsively but harmoniously at the same time with others. "We're about to commence, and you are just on time so, listen very closely and act positively after this meeting as demanded." "We called you here, though you are young, we believe your ears are as broad as the simple leaves." Uncle Jimmy insulted, but that did not make sense to Green at all. "Yes, we don't have to present some sweet preambles in this context, just to say our mind and as well take actions on what we had agreed as a family." Aunty Maggi appeared more hurting, stamping her feet repeatedly. "Hmm… Green, Uncle Ralph called, If you were not rightly intimated by your grandmother, our sister, concerning her properties while she was alive. We are taking over her properties because we helped her some years ago, when she had problems in her late husband's house and came to live with us here. You should know this land is mine, and the lands she cultivated belong to our brother and sister here". "Uncle, please, don't do this to me", Green pleaded. "Shut your mouth and listen to elders; this is tradition", continued Ralph. Uncle Jimmy shouted, and Green started crying silently. "You are now requested to go back to your people; they will take care of you if they want as your father and mother did not have any inheritance here."

"Uncles, please…. Where will I go, and how will I cope? I don't have anybody else than you, and I am a lonely orphan; please help me…." Tears of anguish danced down his cheeks, as he could not help than cry like a child which he was.

"Listen, we can't help you; there is no place for orphans except their parent's houses.

This is similar to the tradition of a female child who cannot inherit any property in her father's house. So, go to your people and let them be saddled with your responsibility," Uncle Jimmy stated clearly to Green. "Yes, that has been our agreement, we only came to tell you to leave. let's go and have some sleep", Uncle Sam concluded, and they walked away. Green was soaked in tears when he returned despondently to his destitute bed after being detruded by his deplorable people, cutting the cord of life that connected them.

In the morning, Green rushed to grandma's tomb to cry the more. His tears stained his rumpled and dusty smelling shirt and short which made him look more unkept as he didn't have a bathe since after grand ma'am's burial. The early morning cool breeze was so passionate and kind to blow towards his direction to help him face his future hurdles.

"Grandma, they have hurt me again because of your departure and I don't have a choice or a place to stay than this place. It seems they are right and justified in their actions because my only family is here". Green lamented.

"I felt deceived every passing day, and you knew about this when you were still alive, yet you couldn't help like my parents. I thought I could count positively on your companionship because you spoke calmly like a friend, yet I still felt everyone was my enemy including you. I must say, there is no place for orphans in this world.

I am disheartened, distinguished among heathens. We are disconnected like umbilical cord between the mother and child and our pedigree may not be remembered at all. There is nothing I can do about it.

Where is safer to stay and make friends than here in the cemetery with graves? I wish I can die soon like you. I have been evicted without reason and consideration. I know being ignorant to a crime may not help sometimes, but why is death punishing the innocent, making truth false? This has become the way of life of most people in the world. I am like an ignorant ventriloquist who stares at scary masquerades without knowledge for survival.

I don't like you anymore, I am not proud of anything because there is nothing to be proud of...."

He cried profusely and rolled on her

tomb like a child with no shame.

"I can see you are buried with your voice, care and warmth. So, I'll cry and call for death until you and my parents answer my questions, or I will meet you there."

Life experience had already cemented Green's relationship with the cemetery before his grandmother's death. He was desolate, weak and had no plans for his life. His repeated yawning could speedily clear some dust particles off the tomb. Still, his weakness compelled strength compulsorily. He ran his eyes on every tree around in seconds to get some food.

Amid tiredness and hunger, hope appeared when he recalled one of the verses in the bible, he was taught in children's class on one of the few days he visited the church with his grand ma'am that says, "give us this day our daily bread…".. Green staggered but courageously, knowing he was in a lonely world that gave no food to the lazy and weak, he tried to be strong but couldn't. He did not remember when he prayed out, "Help me, Lord. Help me please."

In the cemetery, some trees and coconuts branched to each other. The trees were tossed by a wind whose effect was on the leaves. Some squirrels were playing on tree trunks too. Green looked at them and was amazed by the intelligent squirrels who were not relenting in their course of the association at the tree trunk. Green enjoyed a moment of fun, but his mirage faith couldn't get him up for harvest.

In the process, Green dozed off, with his back resting on one of the coconut trees. As he was sleeping, two squirrels jumped on a dry coconut seed stalk in their excited state, and they fell helplessly with the squirrels to the ground. This action surprised other squirrels, and they stopped jumping immediately. The squirrels were weak from such unpredicted fall. One of them moved sluggishly and climbed on Green, who couldn't understand what was happening but cried out while still sleeping.

"Oh… leave me alone. I am not interested."

When the gliding movement of one of the squirrels persisted on his body, he woke up from sleep and shook it off his body. He saw them dancing sluggishly so he killed them immediately. Green was so happy to be blessed with coconuts and meat. He drank the coconut water and ate the fleshly pulp before selling others for some money because he had no food and where to live.

The wind blew steadily through the night and teased softly at humans but created the most beautiful effect on lips and the body as if the winter was finally invading the humid territory without mercy. As the moody early atmosphere unfolded its mysteries, some houses were steamed to ease peaceful sleep. But an older man named Ete Essien, whose blood had never coagulated was not affected by the cold. As he journeyed without a companion to the un-guarded cemetery, wishing earnestly to discuss death for its unabated strength on human especially on him as he had lost his son and wife.

Ete Essien located his son's grave and

dropped his lantern on top of the tomb. He cleared dry leaves and dirt with his bare hands, humming sorrowfully but staggered strongly with maturity at his frustrating condition of having no family at the age of eighty. He opened his bag and brought out a small broom and swept the tomb properly.

"Hmm…!"

"You see, I have done what you should have done for me", Ete Essien lamented referring to his dead son, but he obliged nature for its benevolence, becoming obsoleted and unimportant to his smile in life. "I am the flutist that had nourished nature in all my youthful adventure, drumming and blowing skillfully, sending the mighty to peaceful rest with igniting passionate dreams. But I won't be remembered for long because there is no name for me, and my taproot had permanently been uprooted.

I made the gods enchanted like older men on sniffs but have been alleged and sentenced without words.

What do I glory for at this old age of mine?

Though blessed with baggage, yet no one to welcome me with million smiles. My people say that sons are the only inheritance that could ever crown a man's head. But for me, I would not mind being blessed with a disabled son or blind daughter. Then what happens to me when I breathe my last. Indeed, all my carnivals were a mirage".

He touched the head of the tomb, moving his hand to and fro, whispering.

"My son, I wish I was the one in this position.

I would be exceedingly glad in your

visit with flowers from friends and family.

You have paid nothing to old age.

You shifted ancient boundary.

You have disgraced old age.

How happy are you there with this?

Who would sob for me as I did for my father?

It would have been better to say you had a father.

How would I lay my head when I am gone?

Who would dig my grave?

Who would be bothered how my head is in the tomb?"

He shook his head repeatedly and cried out maturely. In this case, he did not worry about being an elder and crying like a child.

"My ancestors had deceived me; I wish

I did not procreate my kind on earth. Indeed, life is a deceptive drama.

Almighty Father, forgive those evil words of my grief and prepare my days ahead of me, for you are kind and know the best for me, though painful and laborious, I know I am almost home with you; please give me joy in these last days before I sleep finally."

The morning was fast approaching like lightning as he sang his bitter solo. He encouraged himself maturely after a prolonged atmosphere of sad impartation. As he turned to the other end of the cemetery, he was surprised to see a little boy at that time in the graveyard with wet clothes so, he drew closer.

"What do you seek this early morning in the midst of graves son." Ete Essien asked with surprise. "This has been the friendliest place I have ever known and a peaceful home for me," Green responded after some seconds of silence and throwing stones at some tombs. Ete Essien was amazed at such fluency.

"Wow! It seems you are more experienced in this tragedy –my son," The old man wondered aloud.

"Tempters don't get blessed after their temptations, but those tempted passes through a harrowing, awful, fearsome and wonderful experience. I am not smiling – Green reported.

Hmm, And I never find it funny, son. Ete Essien interfered. "It's rather unfortunate that life is not worth living for, and I know nearly all positive thinkers are blessed after each temptation because mistakes during enticement are corrected and used as a positive tool in life experiences, as you've said.

Though it creates new victories after scars but to whom do I celebrate this fearsome glory? Ete Essien questioned and sat with Green on the same tomb.

"It is obvious I had been exposed to this misery and emptiness with nobody to smile with. Green complained.

No problem Pa, Green assured. It is true life is full of failures, and I am among those failures. Green conversed negatively. No…, Ete Essien smiled admirably, stamping his foot.

"Failure could be a motivator if you stand strong and fight, but when your failure effects did not influence your thinking for strength, then you are bound to be a fool forever even when you pray. Son…" He created more sensation for Green to look up to him as he continued. "When you are greatly embarrassed by your failure, you will discover your lost crowns, and your nerves will refuse to be at rest while understanding the value of mantles it had lost for years."

"But pa, Green interrupted. I was cradled in shame and tears and never partnered with a smile at length. I have journeyed with death without facial expression for appreciation," Green added.

"Son… Our wisdom book says, "the fear of the Lord is the beginning of wisdom". God is the foundation to all winners, my son. He patted his shoulder and said, be that winner that would profit the world, don't partner with failure for life." Green hissed immediately and looked away. "Why did you hiss?" He asked the young boy softly.

Because the God you have mentioned is not a friend, Green responded angrily. No,

He is the best of friends. I made the same mistake for many years, and I suffered for it even in my old age. He is a good friend indeed. Ete Essien assured. What should I do, pa? Green interrogated though not agreeing to his message. Ete replied to him, know that anger is a map of the fool. Get angry once and get out of its bondage for smiles, be that man that will raise men. Don't you ever forget that life is a battle, and only those with complete armour girded in wisdom for the journey can survive? Life may be your training ground for perfection. Nobody ever ascends the throne without worthwhile preparations. With these and other promising approaches, you will be the most celebrated hero. I am very confident in that, trust me.

Thank you, pa. Green appreciated. Yes, you are welcome. But, son, let's go home now;

the atmosphere is apparent. Ete Essien requested happily.

Pa, my territory seems very close at such I would prefer crawling. The older man laughed freely and continued, troublesome boy. I meant, let's go home now.

Green threw more stones and bursts out angrily. No home, pa. No promises had ever been fulfilled in my life since, but storms of death had shattered my miserable hovel and recompensed me with nothing than tombs. This cemetery is the most trusted and rewarding place for me." Green explained with flooding tears.

"Get up, son, there is more to life even when it presents it's awful face like smoke, suffocating like wild romance, but it will bring smiles later." Chief Essien assured. The atmosphere of mystery was starred, and the old man was captured by the ignominy of death narrated by the young boy.

"Death…" Chief Essien shouted with tears and continued.

"Why molest a child at birth?

Why give him scars that would speak revenge tomorrow?

I believe fervently in fair judgement.

And equity is watchword and guidance."

He dropped his walking stick and whispered softly.

"Kindly change your cruel hearts on the weak for a while so that procreation can take place for more consumption another day because you cannot eat your bread and have it. Can't you see?

Green stood up and walked away while tears of passion couldn't allow the old man to know who he was than to feel deeply sorry for the boy.

"My son…"

"What?" Green shouted with silent tears, but Chief Essien pleaded. "We have the same pedigree though you are too young to be nursed in this ugly experience. Let's go home together; you will understand more later; this place is too sensitive and dangerous to belong." "Don't worry, Pa, I have good friends here, though they don't talk with familiar sounds, I am usually blessed with a smile when we meet." Green refused softly.

"Son…, never challenge the almighty to a fight, for the blind would laugh ceaselessly at the feeble." I know you may not understand. Let's go." Chief Essien pleaded the more. "In my little sense of comfort, I have never been treated unfairly in this cemetery, then why should I leave without saying goodbye," Green added. "Young boy, this has never been a safe place for anybody; you are not insane to be counted as one, wake up and …" "And what glory had this purity in me? Would it not remind me of those rude paths I have walked?" Green remained adamant. "Hmm… son," he walked closer and continued; let's reserve these bitter experiences for facial expression as you have wished, for it appears the atmosphere is too cloudy such that smile will not penetrate the hearts but let me have you settle under my roof for days, the Lord almighty bless you." Chief Essien prayed.

After some seconds, Green tilted slowly, responded and unleashed his heart for the blessing from the old man. He silently packed his belongings after exchanging good eye contact with him and around the cemetery. Green, who was still angry did not observe or care to understand that the old man was expressing a mature silent glee to heart because the underestimated young boy had won a lot of titles in bitterness; such that the best thing to do was to allow his sorrows than to lure him out.

Green was protected in the old man's house though he could not erase his alarming reflections off his mind. He would wake up every night and imagine why his grandmother's image couldn't flash at least in a moment for encouragement. He will think and reflect severally on how life had been unfair to him when he looked at other children in the community, and he made no attempt to have any friend to talk to, rather, he would like to listen to old people's conversation. When going to stream most times, he walked alone, he will not greet and respond to greetings freely but will listen carefully to others who may forcefully talk to him. This unfriendly attitude was not known to the old men about Green because he spoke freely to them, even initiated conversations, and asked them a lot of questions. They noticed that he was a very fast undisclosed learner.

"Hm …, I am still in an awful trance. Grandma, don't be swallowed like my parents, appear, and re-appear, feed my soul with wisdom, and show me good ways to follow and do not forget gracing my heart for the future you once assured. I am a petulant child; can't you see?"

Green lamented loudly after deep thinking.

CHAPTER THREE

At dawn, the birds were awake and made their courageous cheeping which lured people out of sleep. Green awoke early to sweep and perform other house chores. He sneezed and yawned violently with a long chewing stick which fell out of his mouth each time he yawned. He washed his face to enable him to see clearly. Neighbors were graciously alerted with ease to the different mutated sounds from most market women who talked, laughed, and shouted on their way to the market. The same thing happened on the road to farms, stream, and church. They seemed very happy doing this though most times they argued and fought like children without shame. Young people were also rushing to streams. Green was not happy to be greeted or spoken to by the people he met on his way to the stream. This attitude surprised young people who saw him most times interacting with older people instead.

 The whole habitation was busy with a new strength that could cause people to fly, though lazy people preferred not to wake up early to do anything serious.

"Wow...! What a wonderful morning full of smiles that gladdens the heart. It gives more reason to say good morning with smiles to someone like my Green.

"Good morning Green" The old man, Ete Essien greeted with great delight and sat on a cemented pavement with his legs on the sand near Green. "Good morning pa," he responded.

Green, Ete Essien alerted, "every path around the house looks beautiful. You've done well and it is like clearing ancient pathways with good designs that the brave can never overlook. Once again, I like your animated, gusty character.

Pa, why are you happy about just the sweeping I did? Green queried. "Oh! sweeping is an act of design, showing a path to success and..." No, it offers a course to death, grave, just like those residues in the pit", Green interrupted angrily. Not again this morning, the older man informed, not wishing to have Green argue with him.

If I may ask, when could be the most celebrated time to eat unripe fruit? Will eating it in the morning or night change its poisonous fluids from hurting? Green retorted. Son, the intelligent chief inhaled his snot to respond along with the already charmed Green. Well, death is like a consuming fire, consuming without pardon. No, Green nodes his head in disagreement and continued; death is like an earthquake though not seen, but exceptionally hazardous with unpredicted plans, strongly causing no facial expression for unending verbal expressions.

How long have you partnered with death? How long have you shaken hands with it such that you aware of underworld passions? Pa, while in the womb I saw an end in action with innocent peers, I thought I would be better after crossing the walls of the beautiful womb with soothing amnions, but I never knew that I would be selected to face its wrath in the loneliness of soul here on earth.

My dwelling is death personified; can't you see?

Ete Essien dragged the talented death hunter to a nearby farm at the back of his house. "This is where I should be with my brother, born on the same day with the same umbilical cord." "But grasses have covered his face", Green informed. "Yes, grasses have covered our faces because we are childless and there is no one to make those mystery designs you made this morning by sweeping the pathway on our behalf. The older man responded.

Oh, it's a pity, pa.

"It is never a pity Green, because you've not allowed the cool breeze to teach you another path to life that I am trying to teach you." He responded speedily to silent Green's ignorant attitude. The surrounding bush was tranquil and relaxed, breezed at his neglected brother's grave. Green, he continued. Let me pick out grasses from his innocent face and talk and play with him as we used to in the womb many years ago. Pa, I'll help you weed them away; let's go now. No, don't bother, the older man refused. He started removing grasses and decorating the grave though there was no stone for someone else to know where his brother was buried, the old man still knew the exact place. There were no questions or arguments from Green to doubt his actions.

"But we were born as twin hoping to go home together. You deceived me by travelling alone. What would you tell our ancestors while there? Why didn't we discuss this in the closet to get strangers to shamble by the door? Now I stay alone with no young one to play with. Loneliness has become my friend while you, my courageous brother, travelled miles away without words to soften my grievous heart. How do I stretch to see the moon for its beautiful tales, especial now that life has mistreated me? Hey! Surrounded by many trees but no birds sound familiar." Ete Essien paused and looked at Green with more reasons to continue with his hands playing on his fore longed tomb.

"There is nothing treasured or pleasurable like when you were with me. I pray loneliness would take me to the grave to meet you, but when? Our breeds are no more, our breeds are extinct, and there is nothing I can do about it for you". He shook his head and whispered as if he was talking to someone. "So sorry that I have not been here for so long as promised, but I wish I could be here for eternity... more peaceful sleep, my brother."

He stood up and starred at Green. "Son, he called, you are now my twin brother and a king of the new era, forget about your age for our people say: when a child washes his hands clean, he can dine with the great". Green looked at him and said, "I wish you don't die and leave me the way others did because I can't withstand loneliness over again in this world". "No, no... You will certainly change this pedigree someday, my son." The old man encouraged him" Hmm..." Green sighed as if in doubt without saying a word. Once again, thank you for helping me fulfil my long-forgotten obligation of visiting my brother's grave. You are most welcome;

Green responded with a rapid smile as they walked side by side to the house.

At night Green was happy to sleep without thinking about his battered experiences. But while sleeping, he unconsciously launched into a long-expected graceful mood in a dream.

Green was surprised to hear grand ma'am's voice while he was playing along an unknown bush path. "That voice sounds like grand ma'am." Green wondered aloud and glanced speedily about to behold her presence.

"Yes, I have come because your heart is free of grieve for smiles for some seconds", Grand ma'am continued. "Show yourself; let's be friends again." Green pleaded strongly. "I'm behind you." Grand ma'am responded.

Green turned immediately like wind and beheld grand ma'am's appearance. Green was excited and couldn't stop the smiles on his face. "Where have you been? Are we still friends?" Green questioned with interest.

"Your smiles usher friendship
Uniting broken bonds of ages
Bridging gap for longing discussion
More friendship, my son" – Grand ma'am sang.

"You are the source of my happiness
Your face glitters like the sun
The rays from your eyes strengthen me
Now I can glory in your visit
Stay a little longer, please..."
Green requested.

"It will not be long as it were.

Death is friendly when the heart is strong.

Be strong, for more joy awaits your heart."

Grand ma'am assured.

Your presence gladdens my heart

Placing me in another world of comfort

Your presence is like an unstoppable fountain

Now I have a taste of it

Don't return Grand ma'am" – Green pleaded.

"There is only one fountain, my son."

Grand ma'am introduced

"And where could that be seen?" Green questioned keenly.

"You've were exposed to God when you were very young and innocent, while you held no grudge against death and people around. But you became far away from Him immediately you started fighting and imprisoned your mind with anger and sorrow resulting from the death of your parents. Son God loves you; that is why he waited for you and even used death to preach to you. You were too stubborn not to hear God speak from people around you. Grand ma'am preached

Grand ma'am, please put me in the right frame of mind for I am lost. Green pleaded

"Listen, son, amid death, only peace in God shatters fear and heal wounds. It brings a long-lasting smile, she paused, smiled, and continued

"Remember; God is the source, and you had never mentioned him in your discussions. He owns everything and he decides who dies and who stays in his creation" that is why your parents like other people, could not resist the call of death, though it was very painful to the deceased.

I'm sorry, grand ma'am.

Your absence crippled me without hope- Green apologized.

Son do not fight lost battles with your creator; glide on to smile, peace and simplicity, and free your dull heart young king. Focus on the future, make the best out of life for time waits for no one. Go back to God for Jesus loves you, my son."

As Green was about to question Grand ma'am about his parent, she went away smiling.

Wait, grand ma'am, wait. Can I come with you...? And where are my parents? — Green shouted till he woke up and discovered it was a dream. He said to himself, how can the dead preach? Indeed, Jesus loves me if the dead could preach to me. He wondered and pondered at those words

"Oh! I wish it were a reality, I would have known her direction. God, I am sorry; forgive me and switch me over to the right frame of mind. Let me know peace and appreciate the life you have given me. Get my burdened mind away and start a new page in me, for you know me more than I know myself amen." He was so enchanted after speaking with his grandmother in the dream after a long silence.

In the morning, Green performed all

his duties with smiles. He sang melodious solos while the friendly older man observed silently with a keen interest in his charming and appealing attitude but purposefully wished not to talk about it until he was sure because Green could be repulsive in response, especially when vexed.

After some friendly hours of the morning, Green while eating lunch with Ete Essien kept smiling without a known cause, making fun with plates while the chief was still imbibing his brightly calmed attributes closely.

"Pa, Green alerted charmingly. In death, there is God powering smiles to those who would willingly accept to move on. Though hidden, it heals wounds passionately and blesses the heart with lasting peace anywhere. Thank you for the meal and love. God bless you.

Ete Essien's drinking cup with water fell from his hand as he heard him preach God with a repentant heart suddenly. Green hurriedly packed the plates from the table to divert from his questions.

Hey! Hey...! Sit down. Ete Essien recovered from the sudden shock. "Who offered life to you recently and why?" "Life offered itself to me at the appointed time" Green responded politely. I know you have not smiled for a long time now and that can make you older than I. What is wrong? Why the sudden change and why God now? Ete Essien questioned the more.

"God is the fountain of happiness, peace, and smiles. A very present help in times of trouble. However, bitterness and anger had darkened and dealt with my heart for many dubious years. But I have discovered my lost treasures and never will I smash them on the ground again. What is gone is gone." Green proclaimed. I never thought smiles and happiness could visit your locked territory such that you remember a verse of scripters. This is wonderful to hear, Ete Essien said still surprised. I was captured by radiating change from my late grand ma'am's face in my dream. I was so happy that I didn't want to let her go away. She spoke life than death did. She preached Jesus to me, and I was surprised to know God loves me that he can send the dead to preach to me. Now I have peace.

Ete Essien asked, what could this rapid life be, if I may ask? She said that I had missioned negatively for ages without God, claiming to fight with death, losing God that could heal my wounds and bring long-lasting peace to my troubled heart "She went on to say that my few minutes smile and happiness ushered friendship, uniting broken bonds of ages and bridged the gap for our discussion. Then at the end of our conversation, she told me that Jesus loves me.

As he was recapitulating, Ete Essien was very happy, knowing how bitter Green was before. Son, you are really and must richly dwell in happiness for more rewarding responses will come your way. I am so happy that God decided to use what you wished for to preach to you. Indeed, God can do anything. Wow! this is impressive and the first of such testimonies I have heard in all my years on earth. God bless you young king. Ete Essien prayed.

Young king...? Green said in surprise. You are a king to me whether other people see that or not, the man assured. Unbelievable;

Green wondered, especially after recalling that his grandmother had called him young king in his dream. Yes, my son, that is who you are. Orphans like you can become great future kings to change things for good. You need to see that and think differently to win every life's battle.

In the evening, Green tried to repair some spoilt lanterns in the house, he also had to throw some damaged equipment away. He enjoyed the cool, distilled breeze while Ete Essien, who sat close by, was playing with his long chewing stick in his mouth as he was picking his teeth. He stamped his rave walking stick repeatedly and hummed an unfriendly tune, and Green listened and watched him with smiles.

Pa, your song has no arranged beats or

rest. It sounds horrible. Green said with laughter. I know you don't mind as long as you are happy, Green added. Happiness has been my most fantastic companion, and you can testify to that. The older man responded. Yes, that's good pa, Green replied. Remember, you can always join me in my happy world son. Thank you, sir, Green saluted.

"So, are you progressing on the repairs"? Ete Essien interrogated with no chewing stick in his mouth this time. Yea, it's going on well and I will be successful soon. Green responded with a smile while he put more effort into it. Wow! That's great. I thought the lanterns were out of use. "Well, not really; I will improvise skillfully to nurse a good flame". Green responded looking at the older man's direction with interest.

The Chief balanced and carefully dropped his chewing stick on the nearby surface and starred at Green.

"Pa, I guess it will finally work properly tomorrow unfailingly". Green assured. "Wow! That will be interesting as I have waited for some time now and I will hold unto it till I die, just the way my late wife cherished any gift from me. Thanks, son; God bless you.

I have been thinking about some things lately. You told me about how you dropped out of school in class three when your grandmother could not afford your school expenses. She showed positive responsibility, a measure of faith and belief in your future which I must recommend. I am confident you will make the best at every opportunity given to you as you did during death hunting at the cemetery. I will plead with you to welcome schooling again though you have missed four years. You are very blessed and gifted, that is why you understand many things which baffle the elderly. I want you to be very grounded in academics and any other good thing that comes your way. So, let me get your feedback after you have given it a careful thought."

"Thank you, Pa. I will let you know". Green responded. "Thank you for your good work son, God bless you", the older man appreciated. Together, they had an excellent time, discussing into the calm night.

CHAPTER FOUR

Ete Essien who was very advanced in age, was the family head of the Ufon people and was blessed with wisdom and riches. Still, people always wished he had a survivor to continue his legendary lineage. He taught about including Green as his only surviving son for an inheritance because he knew how his curious family will react and treat him when he departs. The fear of exposing the young boy back to darkness and despair when he dies tormented him such that he couldn't interact with Green freely as usual.

The young boy noticed his new attitude, but he intelligently attributed it to old age by politely refusing to ponder on it since he had freed his heart from worries. Instead, he continually accorded him respect and continued doing all the house chores with delight.

Ete Essien purposely sent Green to an event that will take a while because he wanted to discuss with his family about the issue that bothered him concerning Green. "Good evening, my worthy brothers; Ete Essien welcomed and swallowed bitter kola strongly to clear his voice." "Thank you", They responded. There is a catcher that's worth a noble price in my discretion. I want to drop this on the table for discussion and I know your wisdom which is based on our traditions and customs will be helpful. Ete Essien paused and waited for the usual response though they were very expectant but careful, knowing how intelligent he was.

"Your wisdom is un-imaginable

Though it is cagey, we still need more explanations."

Ete Imo pleaded for clarity.

Imo, my brother, I am happy and very assured some people will wear wisdom shoes soon." Ete Essien smiled before he continued. "My life was a mirage for years though I have tried many times to be the man I should be like a king adorned in a purple garment for the throne. The anguish of death had been too close to me with many days of darkness.

But just in a glance of my misery, I identified with a twin brother that makes sense than morning breeze. He offered help more than I expected. I have come to know that love is not all about physical features because beauty can change at old age." Chief Essien paused and continued maturely.

"Indeed, God appeared to me in the form of a boy, presenting joy immeasurably and will send me to my grave a happy and fulfilled person when I die. I know traditions has said so many things that we can use wisdom to live without reading between the lines. And this is one of the sorts." As he was pouring out his heart, he drew his people deeply into the moist atmosphere of reflects.

"My brother," Ikpongke alerted and continued. We know how heavy your heart is, but we wish you cry more for relief and come out straight so that we can behold light at the end of the tunnel." "That is why we're here, and It is true." Etim said. "Yes, Old men cry in wisdom but, your wisdom and abiding atmosphere has been created for positive display. So, get us involved, let us dance together. You are never alone, my brother." Ete Imo encouraged.

"Yes...., it is about my son, Green", – Ete Essien revealed. "And what makes him your son?" Uduak questioned him speedily. "Everything, I mean everything. I want to include him in my inheritance." He responded. How would a servant of no pedigree share in the meat of the nobles? What would that be?" Etim interrupted angrily. "A change of tradition in our days. Uwak answered mockingly. "God forbid pigs becoming pets... have you ever seen a boy become a priest? And if that happens, how will he be refereed to during confession by the elderly? Oh! Perhaps, boy! I have a confession to make. On whose demand will that be made possible? Just know that it will not happen."

Ete Umo challenged and adjusted his seat.

"Listen, my brothers; Green is my son now and a son's inheritance is what he will get. This is my will before I sojourn to the land of the dead. Good enough, you all are blessed and influential as well." Ete Essien concluded.

"Then you will undoubtedly hear water bubbling while sojourning since old age does not respect traditions anymore." Before we forget, we have sent late Ibiok's wife away as tradition demands, since she didn't give birth to a male child. If the three daughters wish to stay, they can stay, or they will remember their father when they grow older." His angry brothers challenged and went home bitterly. They promised to deal with Green when the time was ripe. The situation struck Ete Essien repeatedly as if he would become an active walking corpse to monitor and secure his only companion. For he wouldn't want Green to be exposed again to those deadly experiences after he has embraced peace and smile as the most lasting solution to his destiny.

CHAPTER FIVE

In one of the evenings, Green and the old man after a long lame of silence without went into their rooms to sleep and Green dosed into an adventure in the dream. In his dream, he broke some palm kennels and ate some. As he focused on what was meaningful to him, a man and woman approached him, but he did not lift his head up initially to know who they were, and their voices were not familiar to him.

"Well done, my son." The woman greeted loudly but whispered to the man," He is very handsome". "Thank you", Green appreciated with no concern. "I wish to break with you", she added. "No, you will dirty your clean dress – Green refuted speedily. "Well..., amid confusion, I guess a stranger can be a friend sometimes" – the man introduced and bent softly wishing to see his face. " I may not give proper seat to people with such pleasantries, and it will be an insult to your personality," Green responded but still on the target. "Well, I wouldn't mind hearing our voices blend, the man added.

What's so special about your friendship. Green challenged as he became bored with their intruding questions. "Destiny, just destiny..." The man responded cheerfully, and Green was cautious to understand his offer. "Your audience would do us a lot of good, my son, and we are happy you care." The woman assured. "Then I won't wish to be nurtured by an unknown fountain for its cost would not be friendly". Green ignored.

"Wow! What a wisdom. Light had ushered an eye that would save the whole lineage to come". The man who was surprised continued with pauses. "And the light is innocent as the moon though surrounded by darkness yet could be very friendly to human" The woman completed the sentence and join her hand with the man.

"Light you are implying is abstract and deceptive.

It had never been a friend to me and my world. As such, we don't belong to the same world, can't you see." Green argued.

"Light may not speak like others,
It may not understand its values yet
Maybe many had not sung its praises

like birds with time

But it's worth is enviable and beautiful"
The man praised.

"You are that light, Green" –the woman, informed.

"How did you know my name?" Green carried up his face with surprise. "The air had been one of the most trusted friends than the wind, but it had never stopped giving information to the wise." The man answered politely.

Why mine, what's so special about me to such cruelty like the wind." Green questioned with a troubling mind abandoning what he was doing to focus actively on them. "We are your parent." The woman informed. Green jumped up from where he sat and distanced himself from them.

"Son, we are very sorry and ashamed that our faces had never been friendly. We wished and always longed to have been with you to nurture the quest we started years ago." Green's mother cried.

"You're not my parent, go away from me, or I'll run away from you." Green challenged and moved backwards. "I know we had abandoned the quest we once initiated, and we were ashamed ultimately when you told us that some years ago." His father reminded.

Immediately Green heard the man say that he remembered and was seriously dumbfounded to hear him and re-echo his words. "Could death hear?" He wondered silently.

"Are you truly my parents?" – Green cried.

"Son, we didn't and couldn't try for you, and it is not our fault. Death is the real; we can never argue, no matter our rank or societal status. We only bow to it when our time is up. We left with the same ring we bought because there was no choice to make.

Your tears smashed us down and made us restless, but we couldn't help you. There is no control over death, son.

"You have not acted wisely to my calls. You abandoned and neglected, exposing me to death and its turmoil. Yet I couldn't see it's face to hiss. What did you think about dad when you both were alive mum?" He changed his position as he drew closer to his parents with keen passion and courage as they rushed and embraced him.

"Son, you were depressed and negatively exploited by death. No man or woman can change the course of death. God made it so, and only he can reverse it. I would have deprecated, challenged, and fought for what I believed as always. You allowed anguish of death and loneliness to have cripple your mind and had blocked your vessels from the rapid flow of blood. Then what is life?" His father sympathized.

Let these happen to me, even more, to visit the other side of life soon with you. - Green wished.

Son, life has become your bosom friend than death so you will do more than us. The atmosphere of your reign to our people will be great. You are a king," - His mother praised.

"King to graves, and animals?" Green asked with doubt.

"No, to your people, our people soon."

His father responded.

"Father, what luxury had life shown since I appeared in this world of doom than regrets and deformity.... could this be for kings."

"You will glory in it than we did, for you are destined to succeed. You shall mount on thrones and smiles shall fill your kingdom; people shall pay loyalty to you more than your predecessors – be strong my son." His father encouraged him by patting his back.

"My eyes refuse to wink at vague promises that will never be fulfilled. The world is rough and wicked, swallowing dreams and ambitions." Green argued the more.

"Son, you will celebrate your victory someday, for you are the best of our kind." His parents embraced him again without his consent, and he felt the bond of love he never felt before in his life.

"Father, mother, my eyes are open…".

As Green was eager to express his feelings more, young people who went to stream that morning playing and made noise woke him from his sleep. He was very bitter when he discovered it was a dream as he wished to continue with his debate. Green rushed out of the house to the cemetery immediately as if he was on a suicide mission, promising not to miss the target. He was so expectant to see or hear his parent more. As he entered, the usual rats, ants, cockroaches, birds, and lizard were parading in divisions in and out of different holes, but crickets had not yet resumed their duty of making noise. They paved the way immediately but wondering and pondering at such unwelcomed visitors at that time of the morning.

"Good morning, Green greeted the creatures. Sorry for scaring and scattering your adventures. I missed your company a whole lot, and I am confident you had munch sumptuously without interference for a while. Once again, thank you for always being there for me and guarding my parents against invaders."

As he was discussing, they were calm, spreading their busy eyes on the available food, and they got ready to thresh as usual since Green had not frightened or trot around.

Green sat on his mother's tomb and stared at the cloudy atmosphere whispering and whistling in the air with a low harmonious sound that can cause a sleepier presence. Then, he stood in between the two graves, looked at his grand ma's stone and spoke,

"Tough times had nurtured my heart negatively in the past.

Training the heart to be strong irrespective of age.

Embracing life with all cost

Though I had wished not to survive several times, but I am not fraudulent as before.

A smile had entered my heart recently

I had been fighting lost battles

But it's like the God I hated is wining wars for me with love.

Though I am still waiting to see if he genuinely cares than humans who cannot fulfil their promises.

Like the warmest friend troubles are

loose.

The chains are freed. I think I can be free"

He swept their tombstones and touched the edges severally while he bade them farewell.

Green rushed home to perform his morning chores but to his amazement, Chief Essien had swept the entire compound.

"Pa, I am so sorry for going out without your consent and..... sit down son, Ete Essien instructed him. I was eager to make good designs like this since you came." The older man revealed with a smile. "So, your silent prayers are answered?" Green interrogated while looking at his face full of smile.

"Listen, son; fruitful age begins earlier than expected. It is full of good and toiling memories, rejoicing and comforted when seeing his sons and daughters sit around the table. It is a productive period; full of strength, courage, and enthusiasm, flourishing like morning flowers, sprouting wonderfully like grasses of the rainy season with glory. It covers both sandy and humus soil layers while displaying its dancing prowess on mountain's tops. It sends its roots into rock spores. Wow! Gifted men shamble with their voices since they cannot penetrate with cracking on rocks.

You are a lion, unharmed like the gods, you may smuggle like scumbag but never lost your dignity. Like a deer, you pant for waters, but you don't drink any that comes your way. I wish I have many years to write your tributes.

I know there are so many people that would never survive the waves you had, no matter their ages. But young people who will hear about these experiences from their parents won't understand and may say God forbid. Some people would have committed suicide, while others would have resorted to vices and become a nuisance in the society. But I still believe few would have prayed with their eyes starred up high as if the answers were to fall like dew from the heavens. If you must pray my son, do it with understanding, believe God can, but don't forget that faith without work is dead.

Success could be sown continuously from childhood without perceiving the exact time it will fruition, but you must believe in yourself. I pray steadfastly to testify of thee before I die." Ete Essien paused.

"Death is never far away, but smile seems to separate them from you when you forget about its fears; the heart becomes new. Learn to smile even when all is not well, for people see and describe you according to how you position your face, character, and attitude to things around you. Always say it is possible even when there are no signs of victory. Be very human to know things may not always go as planned sometimes. Living in the past can make your future oblique and past glory blind fools and make them incapacitated to change the future. Most future generations don't need testimonies of the past, but those who are yet to reach such height would benefit from them.

Son, even though things are not working as planned, put on the right attitude and glide patiently for mockers hardly believe in a second chance. On the contrary, take their mockery as fuel to your winning chances, for they will never know when your intruding visitors had long gone for them to use the door again. If you must open the door, be careful of such friendship, they can intoxicate, and you know what that means.

Remember, the way God used your experience with the death of your family members to help you out of sorrow does not mean he makes friends with death. I can only smile and thank God for delivering you.

When you love to solve people's problems and learn to take care of yourself in time, you are wiser and wealthy. So, remember to give out as many you would love to get back but never beg. Give what you can now; do not promise what you can't fulfill. Treat your family best because they are your gift but remember help usually comes from afar in case you need one someday."

Ette Essien picked up his walking stick, looked at Green and continued.

Don't get richer in sin

Time wasted can't be regained.

In all, there is no excuse for failure.

Though sympathy invites but mourning should not last long like a smile.

If you must run, run with the heart of winning.

Maybe with the price not presented at first sight for encouragement.

But be the victor no one can despise even without a prize for prizes don't last but memories do.

Praises may last, but for a short time

Yet values and worth speak calmly like

air for a longer time

They will announce your name before your arrival.

People will wait patiently for you even when you come in late.

The unborn children will rejoice richly in your expanse in the world.

Nevertheless, my son,

Never fight a lost battle and waste time for nothing as you are growing.

 Old age needs energy but don't reserve it doing things for tomorrow for hunger will not respect old age.

Your light will come soon when it's dawn if you can wait in wisdom.

The old man started walking away and later waited knowing Green will say something.

"Your wisdom and advice are very

soothing; I long and wish for more of this always. Thank you very much". Green appreciated.

Son, I cannot withhold wisdom from you, and it is not a material thing that you must struggle to get, it comes on you freely. God bless you, son.

CHAPTER SIX

Chief Essien was so weak that he could not attend social functions, and his seat was empty in every meeting he had with other chiefs and kings. The kings and other known elders felt the pains of his absence, knowing what it could result in, but no one visited him.

Before the forthcoming official meeting that would involve all kings and selected chiefs from the highly rated communities, Ete Essien had planned on what to do without informing Green. However, on that day, he asked Green to represent and contribute on his behalf.

"My son," Ete Essien alerted. "I am with you, pa", Green responded livelily. "The mountain is about to make its journey for the valley to occupy its position." Hm…! And what experience has the valley to with such a vast vacant position; why not focus on its kind for competence and perfect continuity? Green questioned intelligently. Son, he shook his head as he enjoyed Green's intelligence and continued. The mountain had exposed both strength and flaws without hiding dirty linens from the sun. There are other strengths and amazing mysteries the valley has not unfolded in all its life, and the people in their rasp had fallaciously concluded; giving praises to mountains for trillion years even when its values and worth may not count anymore." The older man established.

"My father," he paused with relief. What do these mountain valley issues have to do with me? –Green ask carefully.

Hoo, hoo, the Chief shouted in amazement. "Get up, son, adorn yourself, and you shall climb and invade the highest mountain that they could not in their time."

"Pa, you are very proverbial; bring me down from this height with soothing explanations." Green requested slowly. "Yes, it is because you are a king, and you understood and used them more. Today is the proposed community meeting of kings and chiefs, and you are to deputize me.

"What...!" Green was soaked in fear of facing the grandeur of the nobles because he knew he would not be able to reverse the old man's pronouncement; tears of fear crept his soul immediately.

But, son, I have carefully watched and beheld your credibility. I have swum like fishes without consciousness severally because I know your character, prudency, and sense of judgment in matters boosted my courage on every word you uttered without scrutiny. This is a gift that must be utilized as soon as possible, and it is possible now.

"Pa, this is an unparallel arrangement that has never happened and will not happen this time. Why do you choose to expose me to creed and cribbage games without sample cards to learn from for maturity? Can't you see this is too much for me? I am a suckling, and nobody would believe my report and what will I possibly say in such a place? Green argued.

"There is no point rehearsing creeds when it comes to matters of intelligence, son. You are an intelligent professor, an intellectual ability never tutored. Pick up my traditional head dress and beads and use for identification. Fly like an eagle, humble as a sheep but as bold as a lion. Speak wisdom like the ancients you'd become in years to come. Write a new chapter and let it be known that gray hairs are not what brings wisdom, but wisdom is a gift, and it can be given to anyone, and you are one of them. May the God of wisdom grace your heart; expose you to mysteries which men had never unfolded. Go alone, my son, but kings will bring you back." Ete Essien encouraged with confidence.

"What will I say there and who will welcome me to use my dirty hands and eat with the brave, can't you see? I could be disgraced and sent home immediately. Hmm…! "may I not spit upon your confidence or shame it like pigs because children are treated like trash by the elderly." Green prayed and moved reluctantly. "No....

you will discover yourself soon, bye my son. Ete Essien shouted and prayed silently for the boy.

At the traditional court, kings and chiefs were seated in their different conventional attires like ornamental plants. Green was halted and interviewed at the entrance of the gates. "Hey, young boy! What brings you here?" One of the guards questioned.

"I am here for the meeting" –Green answered. "What...! Which meeting? "So, this place has become sandbags that children or mad people should build grasshopper houses and summersault at their convenience without respect?" - One of the guards wondered. Are you a king, Chief or an elder, and which of the communities had ever appointed children to be their leader or attend sacred functions like this?" Another guard added while others laughed.

"Please, I wish not to be scolded or insulted. I represent a voice that calm nerves and I don't want to speak riddling". Kindly identify this. Green showed the attires he was given. When they saw the attire, they reluctantly allowed him in but wondered seriously what such a young boy would say amid the mighty though he was not afraid. "Well, we will see your return soon". The guards wished and laughed profusely.

In the exalted palace, kings and chiefs of noble births sat with their staffs in their hands filled with enthusiasm and splendor. Green walked in boldly through the doors, knelt and bowed in humility while the preceding king halted immediately, and others were surprised murmuring.

"What do you seek, young friend" king Etim questioned in a calm voice while others waited silently.

"How important and active are the
eyes of the eagles
As far as the shore with beauty
Piercing through like pain with claws.
Winking wonderfully with bleeding
prey from war.
With more courage like the wind
Staggered in the storm with focus."
Green paused a bit and raised his eyes to greet.

Good morning kings of nobble births."

What...! Some kings stood up silently with surprise and sat again.

"Hey son, this is not funny. Why stir

the wind, why not air for peaceful friendship", the presiding king questioned softly, knowing how such atmosphere could be challenging or dangerous for a boy like him.

"My kings and chiefs, we are not ready for this drama, and it will not occur well. We have different seats, and I have not seen his here". "There is absolutely nothing wrong with children learning how to speak like elders. So, let's avoid distraction", Chief Imaikop explained immediately. "Yes, it is very true, and I agree with you a hundred per cent. He has entered does not mean he is staying, and I will want to see where this mirage image will find a bearing. You can continue, young boy." King Richard requested.

Continue what? When did this start that a child will intrude in a meeting of kings, and we clap hands for his achievements? Please go home we don't have time for this. King Mike challenged "We know what to do but we can here him before we take action though I am surprised and would wish to understand such introduction", king Sam pleaded

"Go on young boy", King Etim commanded

"My fathers, Green alerted
When the north wind dribbles and the south gives no help, when dust satisfies than food during travails, and noise and dry smell cause more havoc to generations, men of valor act with speed without thinking for a moment because if they do, It will shock your heart to discover, It has given bruises you will never forget.

It is better for the wise to die like warriors in few battles than weaklings in millions. So, I rather fight with the wind for fear is a tragedy, else the feeble rejoice in shame. Kindly grant me permission to represent my father as he has sent me; I pray thee."

The Chiefs were extremely surprised by hearing such words from a boy with no fear.

"Who is your father?" Chief Udo Usoro questioned immediately and adjusted his falling wrapper.

"A humble man of noble character, from the Land of the blessed; whose seat speak wisdom even in his absence. A man of the people, a noble chief at that". Green presented the head dressing and beads he was given to them. The leaders of that community shook their heads in acceptance, knowing the owner.

"Essien Udo Etok Umo is my father."

"Oh, oh! Now I know the hand that cradled you though children cannot learn this." Chief Imoh said in surprise.

The kings stepped aside and had few minutes discussion. They strongly argued about such accidental adjustment to undisputed traditions for a child and a commoner. But since they couldn't resolve such a matter in a haste, most of them hid their displeasure and allowed him stay promising to see Chief Essien for explanations.

"Yes, it is true that a child that speaks like kings can sit with kings though this has never happened in any Land. My people, I am very sorry for how this has turned out to be. He did not come with a seat, and we do not have any that suits him now, and a woman who gives birth in the marketplace cannot keep rules. So, we can welcome both the baby and mother and forget about where she put to birth, one of the kings spoke proverbially.

In this, I must commend Chief Imaikop for seeing it coming. That we don't have a choice now does not mean we are weak. Tradition is tradition, we will see his father later. "Son, your presence may count positively, sit with us" King Etim welcomed him while others sat calmly still pondering, and wondering.

"Your voice stimulates coagulating blood through the marrows. Thank you, my kings, and chiefs, may you live long, Green appreciated, and sat on the floor close to the wall and listened.

My kings and chiefs let's go back to our discussion. What should we do to the people of Abang Iba for disobeying our orders? As for the issue of female children, we cannot bend our customs and traditions. The presiding king stated and opened the floor for discussion.

"Thank you very much my worthy king, for the kola nuts; they are very fresh. A child that doesn't allow his mother sleep will not sleep either. Let's wage war against those that disobeyed; as for the women or girls' issue, our traditions have already provided answers as you have said" -chief Ibanga contributed.

"The sluggish pace of the tortoise had never prompted sleeping on the road. We have exercised patience more than enough, but all they deserve is trouble. King Akpakpam added. To make hay while the sunshines does not imply we should prepare haphazardly. But let's finish this before the sun rises at Abang Iba community. Allow women to manage the Kitchen in their husbands' houses. King Udoma concluded.

I greet you, my people. King Ubo started slowly. It is not something we should lack answers to at any time; our traditions see women as week, helpers, wives if married, mothers if she has given birth but hates unwanted pregnancies and calls such children illegitimates. The gods of our Land have forbidden us and commanded us to treat women as they have instructed, and we have been acting rightly to their instructions. So, this topic is invalid, except we have gone out of the ways of the gods, thank you.

Yes, that's true. All the leaders accepted his explanation and were satisfied and could hardly say anything further on how to treat women.

Oh, Ete Iwat Ibreke. Chief Iwat called angrily. Are we too insignificant in their eyes? Who are the challengers? Let us frustrate and dethrone their king immediately. Hmm...! That may work but not completely. Their people may refuse to be bothered about our actions, which will make us angrier because they have the right to select another king for themselves. King Green Ukpong exposed.

Most of the kings and chiefs who were most prominent were proposing to destroy the Abang Iba community and they were murmuring angrily.

"My kings," Green alerted with his hand in the air. "Please, I wish to make a contribution" You can continue, my son" king Etim responded but others murmured and wondered what he would say while some were so angry to have him there at the meeting.

"Thank you." Green stood up and continued. "No, you are not an exception. Sit down and talk." King Etim informed. "My fathers, I wish to stand to show respect, honor and never to play equality with the gods. Thank you." Green refuted politely.

"I know I am not the right person to say this and Chief Essien my father did not discuss any of these issues with me before, but I guess my voice can be heard. With an apology to all my father's here, I want to believe that most of you are all orphans now, but you and your children are not maltreated. You are all royalty given birth to by women irrespective of their sizes and backgrounds. You do not hate them, but you celebrate them always, even in their deaths. Every female child is a child just like a male, whether from royalty or not. How will you feel if your princesses and princes are pursued out of your kingdoms because they are orphans? I guess orphans are humans, whether free-born or slaves. Are we orphans in any way? Have| we been ridiculed? Who among these groups are illegitimate? The parents who brought the children without planning or the innocent children who came by them without a choice? If women can give birth to royalty, then what is royalty without women? What is the striking difference or features of a commoner and the throne apart from the crown? What is the value of the throne without the commoners that will cheer the crown? The crown does not speak to heights but commoners. Commoners are the strength of every throne. I think it's only possible for royalty to rule over the commoners, not another royalty. Commoners are as crucial as royalty, though they are not royalty but if they revolt and make themselves royalty, they are royalty because they can choose especially when their pains are unbearable."

"What...!" Some chiefs shouted in amazement. "My son, wait, let me think about your message for a while" King Green Ukpong who was one of the kings pleaded and continued. "My brothers, I know what I heard, and my ears are not blocked. In all my life, I have heard children speak but not this way. He said these "If our children are pushed out because they are orphans, what will we do in our graves? And "if commoners should revolt against royalty and make for themselves royalty, I believe nobody will be able to oppose them because they are right" I think this is a voice of reasoning because we all are orphans and most of us ascended our thrones as orphans given birth to by women". Let me help you my brother because I know what I heard. Please don't go too far, king Green Ukpoung, I, king Uforo have not seen my mother, the late queen of Idiong kingdom. So, I am an orphan born by a woman? Wonderful, my son. Thank you, he concluded.

Yes…, Most of us are sons of palace maidens when our fathers couldn't bear a son from the queens; others were not born in the palace because some of our fathers had affairs outside, what about the case of marrying king's daughters to become kings? My son, continue, for the gods sent you, or you are a different god yourself. Most of the monarch responded and supported his contribution before Green continued.

"Please let us think again, cherish, respect, and protect our girls and women, rewrite some pages that need to be written, and make our lands, values, and traditions a dwelling place and hope for our people. Thank you, my fathers". Green appreciated. They all calmly reflected on what he said and nodded their heads.

"Secondly, my kings, it is a pity that the people of Abang Iba had brutally stepped on our toes heavily for this long and caused blisters and fractures to the bones as I have learnt in this meeting". Yes, it's true. They responded. "But why should we glory in a river, so turbulent with ambiguous contents yet it possesses an abundant peace we can't comprehend. Why drink of it with a dark-colored cup, closing our eyes in deafening comfort? How would satisfaction be achieved without consciousness? Though it quenches taste now, won't regret visiting us in the future? Tell me, how will we receive its bitterness at old age? And what will we tell our children when they ask? I can see the frustration on their faces".

They were all overwhelmed with what they heard from the young boy. "My son, you are blessed with wisdom, knowledge and discernment". King Usung Uwem said.

"My fathers, let us not alter traditions because I know most of us are grandsons, uncles, stepfathers, and most of all in-laws in the Abang Iba community. Then why should we bite the fingers that fed us and go free?"

"Hey! Alligator peppers are ripened on virgin grounds", the first elder said and swallowed bitter kola to clear his throat. "Warriors are useless when wisdom is deafening", King Mike lamented. Most of the chiefs could not sit down again. " shame to infidels that ignore the chipping sound of small birds, king Akpan shouted. At the same time, others sat down despondently shaking their heads with overwhelming joy.

"Please, does the community in question depend on other communities among us for survival?" Green questioned calmly. Yes, timbers, cocoa, palm wine, bamboos, raffia, fishes etc. They chorused hastily.

Then why do we scratch ourselves like scumbags pretending to maintain cultured protocols? Green paused and continued.

My humble suggestion is, Let us withdraw these privileges without protest, and they will run back to their source pleading. We can welcome them with cautions and conditions to see their true submission since they cannot survive without these. With this, we will not stain our hands and alter the traditions of our valued lands. Thank you". Green rested.

The kings and chiefs were so happy, applauded him with a standing ovation. One of the kings made space for him to sit with them immediately because he was sitting on the floor initially.

"Please, my father's, this is not for me. This is for royalty, and I don't know why I am here". He pleaded with tears of joy.

Son,

You came as innocent as a saint

Running away from scumbags.

Like virgins abhorring night plays

We are enthused and we celebrate your

splendor, Son of the nobility

King Green Ukpong praised and bowed.

Wow! Withdrawing privileges! Just that and

these vast problems are solved. Chief Ebuk

smiled, clapped, and bowed the more.

I didn't know, and I wouldn't dream

that a child could be the very eye that searches

mysteries to lead the aged. Oh! My days of

ignorant were alarming without your kind to

pull me out of its crux. Thank God you are

here now acting so pleasurably, igniting our

strength and making our moment colorful.

King Green Ukpong said.

"Some destinies are clearly seen, while

others are blurred. I have not seen you sit

reluctantly in wait for yours to grow, but you

are on it already. I cherish your courage, young king. Our people in all Land must hear about you". King Udoimo appreciated. Yes, they will; you must come from another royalty for such has never been seen among commoners – you are significantly significant. Chief Udo gave him a friendly handshake.

The whole palace was filled with the most recent comedic appraisal with no director to connote its roles, yet every participant acted skillfully with the indwelling atmosphere,

It seems we had been energized such that our congeal blood had diffused actively like young men during their games.

Later, Some kings gathered and whispered to each other, and other chiefs waited silently for their return.

"So sorry for the delay." King Etim apologized. Excuse me, My king, Chief Udoakwa interrupted. "I'm sorry to interrupt you. Anyway, it's a matter of importance that my mouth wishes to speak." "Then let your heart not be restrained or befuddled. Speak, let us yearn for its mysteries." King Etim replied. "Thank you," he appreciated and continued.

"My son, he paused passionately. What is your name? Tell us a little about your pedigree since you've been with the mighty. Chief Udoakwa rested. Oh! It's true, very accurate, go on, my son, king Etim, affirmed.

"I am a son to nobody but death", - Green started. "I have no father or mother so; I am an orphan.

Please, tell us who you are in explicit

terms; orphans have roots. Chief Udofa pleaded softly. "I am an orphan who had not seen a father or mother... Tradition and customs of our great Land hate us just like female children" He paused and stared at them for a while. I am Green. That's my name.

He cleaned tears from his eyes while king Green Ukpong adjusted immediately on his seat, looking at him with keen observation. Green, my son, are you from this community? For Chief Essien's wife and son died many years ago – chief Udofa questioned closely? "My late grandmother, Mmayen, is from this community, but my late father was from the Edemanam kingdom".

Eh........!

King Green Ukpong shouted and jumped up from his seat straight to Green, but the nobles did not understand such rapidity.

"My son", he held Green.

"Please, what was his name?" King Green Ukpong asked consciously? "Udoenang was his name"- Green responded with flooding tears. Oh!   Udoenang Green Ukpong Green.

King Green Ukpong shouted and cried with his two hands hemming Green with more tears while others were still watching them with surprise. As the proud king looked at Green's face, he recalled those memorable experiences he had with his late son, Udoenang, Green's father.
Green,

"Green Udoenang Green Ukpong. That is who you are, the noble king of my kingdom. I am your grandfather. King Green Ukpong exposed". "No, leave me alone, it's not true. I have no living family member since my parents and grand ma died".

The noble kings and chiefs were drawn deeply into the situation with clear understanding, became emotional and some of them were shedding tears unknowingly. Nobody could pretend anymore as they listened to the young boy's story and the pains he had suffered on account of traditions which did not favor the orphans, widow, girls and women.

"My son and king", king Green Ukpong called. "I have been busy in ignorance and clouding mistakes. My selfish attitude could not allow me an audience to your late father, my son, such that he was buried in a strange land. He was so egoistic like me and proudly walked away from my presence, despising royalty, and traditions to marry a commoner. But I didn't know a king had been born in my stead. I lost him forever because of our beliefs and tradition. So, get up because your tears are over. I decree today in the presence of noble kings and chiefs of every land in this meeting that my kingdom will be the first to crown a boy king, and he will do all that he shared with us in this meeting".

"When loved ones which you cherish a lot refuse to pay homage or smile with you on an important day of your life, you feel considerably deserted, rejected, and unimportant because they are those to sing your worth. I have been brutally hooded in agony, but I had never imagined or hoped- for this day". Green complained.

"Son, you have indeed taught us

wisdom and opened another chapter in every kingdom. You've been significantly refined through this awful process though too young to partner with death experiences, but you are chartered with knowledge, and we are proud of you. Please let this be likened to wordplay or comedic appraisal for relief – chief Udofa pleaded with much concern. My son, let royalty be corrected by your gifts, for I had never imagined a child could save generations like you have done today. Your late father will be proud of you. Now let it be chronicled that orphan are no more slaves, slaves are humans like us, commoners are the same as free born because they are the strength to thrones, and both women and girls are the best gifts just like boys and men. Thank you for blessing the traditions of our Lands. May God bless your reign than ours". King Etim concluded.

Amen, all the kings and chiefs agreed unanimously. They waited for king Green Ukpong and his grandson to bond.

I love you grand Pa. Green smiled. I love you too my son- king Green Ukpong responded.

At the end of the imparting meeting, all the chiefs and kings greeted Green and prayed God's favors to grace his kingship and the monarchs were delighted to pass the message to their kingdoms.

His grandfather was so happy to have a vibrant and fabulous grandson filled with wisdom as a king and requested the kings and chiefs to join him and pay homage to Chief Essien.

"Pa...., there is an entourage by your door; come and see them outside". Green called on Ete Essien from the inside. Ete

Essien came out and embraced all the kings and chiefs, sharing smiles and laughter.

Green stood beside his grandfather and continued "In the midst of it all, God has whispered peace and smiles which radiate to the wounded hearts, bringing an enduring hope to people. Just as you had prophesied, the same is with me now. Here is my grandfather, king Green Ukpong Udoenang". The traditional title men laughed merrily at the young king's effort. Well, at least my son had said something, the grandfather appreciated and walked towards Ete Essien.

"Now that I know with certainty the precious root you emanated from, I can die a fulfil death. Thank you for blessing old age. May God bless you than kings my son, Essien prayed, and they responded Amen.

King Green Ukpong embraced and

thanked chief Essien for his fatherly coverage for his grandson and promised to hold his gesture in high esteem.

Green moved to his hometown and joined his people with merriment. His name and wisdom spread like wildfire to different kingdoms by the monarchs who longed to have such a prince. His grandfather crowned him king at a young age like he said and assigned elders to teach and guide him through the culture and tradition of the Land. The people of Edemanam kingdom were so happy.

Young people were enthusiastically bragging and glorying in the young king Green Udoenang Ukpoung. His splendor reached and made many kingdoms to respect girls, women, widows, orphans, and commoners. However, it also made young people responsible as they took over leadership positions because the elders started seeing them as the best for the future.

CHAPTER SEVEN

The people of the Edemanam kingdom gathered and waited for their new king to address them as tradition demanded. "My people, King Green Ukpong, his grandfather introduced. "Idung isongo," he chanted. "Iya," the people responded happily. "Idung Ukpong isongo;" he chanted. "Iya (they responded)."

It is a blessing to share kola in happiness. The hind limb of goats follows the exact pace of the fore-limbs, and the river that empties into the stream did not make a mistake. Then let the proud chicken pant for the strength of hawks may be aversive. Our eagle has arrived with unprecedented glamour, in a way it has never been done anywhere. A big welcome to all the kings and chiefs of different kingdoms who love us and identify with greatness. I solemnly greet you. With no further ado, welcome our very own king Green Udoenang Green, the first and youngest king to ascend the throne in any kingdom." The people shouted, waved their hands, and applauded the young king.

"Thank you, my father. I am loyal to you. Thank you, royal highnesses and chiefs of fabulous kingdoms who came to see this once orphan now a king. It is a great privilege which I never dreamt of or prayed for. Thank you".

"It's good to identify with smiles and
It's good to be home.
It would not have been else way than

this proud kingdom of nobility whose credibility is unsearchable.

You are the throne that I treasure and the seat that I am confident to sit on. Some seats may harbor hatred, but I am confident, you will instruct in love, because we are in for the very best, we will cherish everyone, even those yet unborn. We are the foundation and we lay it from now.

What a home filled with strength that brings unity, a unity that nurses hope, hope that tomorrow is in today with smiles, then we live for tomorrow because we are in today. We are in a world where everyone is equal. In my small years of experience, I have passed through some tough times like most of you had because of certain songs of Neglect against orphans, widows, women, girls, slaves, and commoners. This caused serious problems and death to people and damaged our lands because of certain traditions we inherited without scrutiny. Not all traditions are evil but there are some that we must rethink and rewrite for peace, comfort, smiles, friendship, and love to reign in our lives and community.

We are in the world where everyone is or will be an orphan, either now or later. I know these songs have crippled many people, families, and communities, but we are all orphans irrespective of social status because our ancestors are no more alive." The people cheered happily.

"I will treasure and defend the course of every citizen with complete respect to equality and worthwhile culture to the free born, boys, girls, women, slaves, commoners irrespective of family, clans, class and tradition. My ears will be very open to any kingdom and people that needs my help. It is time we love each other; it's time we see ourselves as one. It is time we build a united family, a peaceful society, a treasured city, a joyful nation, and a loving world that will not judge people's skin, situation, language, social status, and gender.

In this kingdom, orphans are not slaves; slaves are human beings like us, widows are mothers we loved, boys, girls and women are the treasures we must cherish and protect. Fathers must be respected as well. No more abuse and discrimination, no more songs of Neglect and let equality become our new call. Let brothers-in-law and families of the deceased be careful in their judgment of widows, widowers, and their children, for the king will not smile at bad judgment that makes them suffer and sing songs of neglect. Henceforth, we will not sell our daughters to their husbands in the name of bride price; neither will we give them out for free as prisoners for a death sentence. This kingdom will prosecute in-laws that lay their hands or maltreat our daughters. We will not condone our sons who do the same to their wives from another land. Let us train our children properly to avoid vices, shame, abortion, and unwanted pregnancies.

If an unwanted pregnancy happens, we should not throw them away or send them out to more danger. Let wisdom be profitable to direct. Young people are to be actively involved in politics and aspire for greatness not to become destructive vehicles anymore. Our parents must see our greatness before they die a happy death.

In my past, hatred was for death, and the future is unity, love, and equity. Know this, your love and hospitality would not impair my judgment. My words are documented by the decree of King Green Ukpong Akpabio Atad Akpade Green the 5th and his grandson king Green Udoenang Green Ukpong Akpabio Atad Akpade Green the 6th for active pursuance of the good and safety of our people and land. Therefore, for other kingdoms who embrace this course to end bitter traditions as we do, my father, the king of this land, king Green Ukpong Akpabio Atad, salutes you. And we will make our Lands the next Paradise on earth".

"Long live the king." The people repeated and clapped

"Long live the queen." The people shouted and clapped

"Long live princes and princesses of this kingdom."

"Long live the blessed kings of our lands."

"Long live my people, long live our noble kingdom." The people shouted and applauded.

"Long live the kings and chiefs of other noble kingdoms whose warm embrace and prayers I will never forget. Thank you for making me feel like a king on that memorable day before you even discovered I was royalty" The Kings and Chiefs from different kingdoms raised their staff in recognition and concluded that the ceremony was very inspiring for a boy to have such an entourage in his tenth year.

"May God almighty bless you. "No more songs of neglect. Thank you." The people applauded him repeatedly and echoed, "No more songs of neglect…."

Most matured men and adults pondered on his statement because he was not speaking like a child.

"…songs of Neglect must stop, equality is our new call… but tradition will speak positively for people in soft tones". What a boy and a massive change! some people commented in the audience.

The ceremony ended with lots of refreshments for the people. Still, his words were lively repeated in the mind of the intelligent to show the kind of king he would be without inequality and favoritism, to add positively to tradition and intelligently correct some in wisdom not to alter them. Kings and most chiefs who saw him at the meeting attended his coronation and were so happy to share in the new dreams that will bring lasting peace, love, happiness, unity, and blessings to their people. They prayed for him and advised his grandfather, the king, to groom him properly.

At the dining table, the royal family had discussion. "My father", Green, alerted while the palace maids were discharging their duties in front of the king. I'm all ears, my son- his grandfather responded.

"I wish with humility that we should visit the cemetery for old memory and pay our respect to my late parents, or should I do that alone for the family?" Green asked. Son, you are a true king with wisdom, romanticized in beauty and your purple robe will ignite your people to respect royalty with enthusiasm. We'll go with you". King Green Ukpong accepted.

"Thank you, my king- the young king praised".

"Hey…! See what I had missed from birth; his grandmother sympathized and offered a speechless smile". "Not anymore". Green assured.

At the cemetery, Green showed his grandfather the graves as he recalled his lonely and tragic past and those frightened animals that were like his housemates. He shared his experiences with his grandparents.

"Son, king Green Ukpong touched the head of the tomb. You are a victor, a philanthropist, a man of courage, believing in what men had not seen, though you died without seeing your belief, it is viable, and the world cannot resist your confidence now. Your seed is on the throne speaking your vision. I'm indebted. I am so sorry that I didn't get along with you as I should have. But I am enthused by your wisdom. I love you."

"Dad, mum and grandma. Your words had germinated", Green recalled and smiled.

You know I have much to say but not like before. I am grateful to God that I can smile, I have a home and a family. I said many things in the course my stubbornness in the past. I thought I could challenge and make war with death, but I ended up chasing the wind. Now I know everything happens for a reason and for the good of those who love the Lord.

All the trouble I passed through, opened the way for my people and brought change willingly without a fight. I learnt in the process that it is foolishness to fight with your creator. Your words have survived all the environmental factors like viable seeds. Dad, your throne is secured, mum, your seat is lonely but very hopeful, though it may take long, and grandma, smile has completely dominated my heart like you said.

We pay homage with good tidings withholding nothing. You are alive because your memories live with me. Songs of Neglect is no more in this kingdom. We are one. I love and miss you". Green spread-out beautiful flowers around the tombs while the frightened animals adjusted into their hiding places for safety. Meanwhile, the palace secretary wrote down king Green's true story while Ete Essien gladly sent in his insightful story even when the young king was not aware of his secret writings about him.

ABOUT THE AUTHOR

Owonam Umana Ebong is an MBA student at the Anglia Ruskin University Cambridge UK. He has taught in some secondary schools in Nigeria after obtaining a bachelor's degree in biology education from the university of Calabar. He is happily married to Inibeghe Ebong.

Printed in Great Britain
by Amazon